I *voted* for BIDDY SCHUMACHER

mismatched tales from the mind of
Brian Centrone

featuring photos by luke kurtis

To everyone who cast their vote for Biddy.

This victory is for you.

Also by Brian Centrone

Erotica
An Ordinary Boy

Also from New Lit Salon Press

Retrospective by Michael Tice

Southern Gothic: New Tales of the South
edited by Brian Centrone and Jordan M. Scoggins

Behind the Yellow Wallpaper: New Tales of Madness
edited by Rose Yndigoyen

Salon Style: Fiction, Poetry & Art
edited by Brian Centrone

Startling Sci-Fi: New Tales of the Beyond
edited by Casey Ellis

Many thanks must go to all those who have assisted in the editing of these stories over the years, but especially Sandra Taurisano, Claudia Stuart and Carey Parrish.

I would also like to acknowledge the Editors of *Voyages*, *INK.* and *Red Rover* for publishing the stories originally. I was honored and humbled then; I am honored and humbled now.

My complete gratitude to Jordan Scoggins, this book would not have been possible without you.

Praise for the e-Book edition

"With the fewest of brush strokes, Brian Centrone hauntingly crawls into the psyches of the characters he creates producing whimsical, absurd but deliciously relatable short stories."
—Arthur Wooten, author of *Arthur Wooten's Shorts*

"From the righteous, puritanical Biddy to the chain smoking, suffocated Emma to a man seeking an exit from his meaningless life, the characters in Brian Centrone's stories face the world with both indecision and decisiveness, honesty and self-denial. Electing to read *I Voted for Biddy Schumacher: Mismatched Tales from the Mind of Brian Centrone* is easier than voting for president—though, of course, one should do both! Centrone evokes the frustrations of Nora Helmer, the blind certainty of the flock, and the ennui of post-adolescent adulthood in three funny, somber, and existential tales."
—Lacey N. Dunham, editor *THIS Literary Magazine*

"A varied, entertaining collection … I'm voting for this e-book."
—Chris Killen, author of *The Bird Room*

"Good things come in three, and so do Brian Centrone's stories including in his newest collection, *I Voted for Biddy Schumacher: Mismatched Tales from the Mind of Brian Centrone*. Each story intrigues, delights and leaves readers begging for more. A short but eye-opening read, Centrone's collection of shorts is the book one goes to bed with, at the end of the day."
—Alina Oswald, author of *Journeys Through Darkness*

"This is solid, engaging stuff—the work of someone who clearly knows what he's doing. I look forward to a novel-length work!"
—Brent Hartinger, author of *Geography Club*

TABLE OF CONTENTS

The Life and Times of Biddy Schumacher:
A Fantastical Story

vote BID
SCHUMACH
OFFICE of DISTRIB

Biddy Schumacher could remember precisely the day she ran for the Office of Distribution in Hills Valley. She woke up that morning feeling queasy and chalked it up to nerves. As usual, in one big sweeping motion, Biddy tossed the covers off and, as if mounting a horse sidesaddle, sat upright on the edge of her single bed. She took a firm hold of the water glass that sat all night on the compressed wood nightstand she had purchased at a rummage sale the Methodist church in town had thrown. She hadn't an urgent need for such a nightstand; she had inherited a worn out, olive green and rusted iron snack table from her mother—may God rest her soul—but she bought it in a show of good faith, friendly neighbor-ism, and a more general, "I don't hate you because you're Methodists and will burn in hell for all eternity since we all know Catholicism is the one true religion" show of solidarity.

Sipping the lukewarm water, Biddy swished the tasteless liquid around in her mouth before swallowing. She plunked the glass down hard, stretched her arms, and made a little moan as she slid her feet into her well-worn powder blue slippers. Then, she stood up, smoothed out the wrinkles in her vertically striped pajamas—white with brown, red and mustard—and strode enthusiastically into the bathroom. She shut the bathroom door, locking it behind her. Biddy respected her privacy, even when alone. She did her business in the dark, for she didn't care to be witness to nature's call.

When finished, she walked from the bathroom—which sat in the middle of her only hallway—to her living room, rounded the coffee table and bounded into the adjacent kitchen, ending her repetitious path. Some would say Biddy's home was small, though she might choose to call it quaint or cozy or, if entertaining a guest, both.

Once in the kitchen, she set about her usual routine of preparing her morning coffee. When Biddy was little, her mother—may God rest her soul—insisted on making tea instead and raised Biddy on the pale brown liquid in an attempt to make herself and her only child more cultured. "Coffee is for everyday people," her mother said. "Tea is for extraordinary people," and poured the steaming drink into fine bone china cups.

As Biddy grew older she became less inclined to drink tea. Coffee became a better choice because, after all, it was her own choice and, since becoming her own woman at the ripe old age of 32, decided she felt just like everyone else. On her very first trip to the grocer she placed in her cart the very first can of coffee ever to touch her strong hands: A fine Colombian roast, with a man and a donkey on a blue tin.

Since then, Biddy had touched countless cans of coffee and drunk down enough of the dark drink to keep the man and his donkey smiling for years to come. She savored the smell, allowing it to perk her up, as she did that very morning before boiling a pot of water for her oatmeal. It wasn't always oatmeal that Biddy boiled water for; sometimes it was for eggs. On those occasions she also browned some left over potato wedges in the toaster oven—also inherited from her Mother, may God rest her soul—which had constantly been used to cook salmon. Biddy did not carry on that tradition either. In full rebellion, she never graced her home with anything that swam as a way of living.

When breakfast was consumed, Biddy washed, dried, and put the dishes and pots away. She took the same repetitious path to her bedroom and proceeded to get ready for her bath, placing on her soft, well-worn terrycloth bathrobe—red, with a black stripe running down the left side. She had bargained for it at a bazaar set up by the town's Jewish community in order to help raise money for their pilgrimage to the Holy Land—as if that would spare them the fires of hell.

After filling the tub with water, Biddy tossed in a few scented bath beads she had once received for Christmas from an acquaintance at work. In truth, it was more of a Secret Santa present than a random act of holiday cheer. Nonetheless, Biddy was quite taken and very satisfied with the bath beads and only used them on special occasions such as this. That same Christmas, and for the same reason she bought the nightstand, Biddy had purchased hand decorated potholders in a Kwanza theme from another charity sale. The holders were given to Padma, the only Indian woman—as in, Ex-British Empire Indian—in the office. Biddy had later found out that Padma meant lotus dung and felt sorry that the woman had been given such an unfortunate name.

As Biddy soaked in her bath, she reflected on the Secret Santa gift she had gotten the year before the bath beads. Biddy never did fancy the 365 day-a-year gardening tools desk calendar and used it as scrap paper in substitute to its original purpose. On each day she would make little notes to herself such as: Water the Cactus, turn the couch cushions over, de-crumb the toaster oven, and run for Office of Distribution. That last note, which featured a lovely image of a weed puller, had gotten misplaced for the duration of a year and a half, and was found, as luck would have it, just in the nick of time for Biddy to throw her name in the pot with the other well intentioned, yet less ambitious townsfolk. She found it under a stack of *The Awakening* magazines she graciously accepted from soliciting Jehovah Witnesses on Saturday mornings and saved for a period of time she felt was appropriate before burning them—as the solicitors themselves would burn for not being Catholic.

When she was as clean as she believed she could get, Biddy toweled herself off and went about choosing her clothes for that day. Wrapped up in her robe, Biddy fingered her way through her closet. She chose a pair of black slacks and a scoop neck floral print blouse in white with blue, cream, and peach. Black flats and support hose completed the ensemble.

Biddy brushed and blow dried her hazelnut colored boyish bob, affixed 14kt gold ball earrings to her lobes, and applied just a touch of rouge to her cheeks, forehead, and nose. A quick spritz of her favorite eau de toilette, Jean Naté, and Biddy was ready.

The day was sunny. A cool breeze swept in from the west as Biddy walked to the Town Hall, where the election would be taking place. She stopped every couple of feet to smell the various flowers growing in the well-manicured lawns along the way. Hills Valley was a pleasant town with a population of four thousand and sixty-two—soon to be sixty-four—when Marybell Grossenthrop née Fingerling had her twins. Two girls, Doctor Needleman had said, but then again, it was the same doctor who told Mrs. Eloise Fitzburge that her husband was suffering from acute appendicitis, when in fact it was just very bad gas from the onion bhajis Mrs. Eloise

Fitzburge made in an attempt to make Padma feel more at home, being the only Indian woman in the town.

Mrs. Eloise Fitzburge had thought that Padma, being single, might take an interest in her son, Seth, who, even his mother couldn't deny, had not even been an attractive baby. However, to Mrs. Eloise Fitzburge's displeasure, Padma actually had standards and her relations with Seth never went beyond their first introduction. Interestingly enough, Biddy had always taken a liking to Seth and found him to be quite charming, despite his deviated septum-induced nasalness, bugged-out eyes, and acne-scarred, pasty skin.

Biddy, not being the forward type when it came to men, and Seth, not being anything at all, never made their way towards each other, even though their greetings lingered on for more than what was acceptable politeness.

Nearing the Town Square, Biddy could see the steeples of Hills Valley's four churches—Methodist, Catholic, Lutheran, and Baptist. The only other two religious houses—one synagogue, Temple Emanuel, and the Kingdom Hall—were not traditional looking establishments. The latter was built out of a converted one-story house/basket shop that had sadly burned down one evening three years earlier. The fire could have been avoided, the Fire Chief explained, had there not been so much dry wood in the place.

Town Hall, like the four churches, was a white clapboard-sided building plop in the middle of the square. It had two stone slab steps in front without a railing. There was once a big town meeting to discuss the addition of railings to the steps, but the idea was shot down because the iron posts would have to be drilled into the steps and, being the original pieces of stone the town was founded upon, could not be fathomed by anyone in Hills Valley.

Biddy smiled brightly as she entered Town Hall. Her queasiness had disappeared and was replaced with a sense of serenity. She attributed this to her optimism that she would be elected this day. Of course, it could have also been the heavy bowl of oatmeal that still sat in her stomach.

Walking up to the ballot box, Biddy ticked her name off on the crookedly cut slip of paper, folded it in half, dropped it into the old wooden box, padlocked for security and accuracy, and posed for the camera in the town newspaper's attempt to capture the moment. Later on, Biddy would frame the photo, which had made it into the paper, and place it on the nightstand. It became the last thing she looked at before bed and the first thing she looked at upon waking.

It was a long wait for Biddy. The election took most of the day, and the counting took most of the night. Finally, just when she thought she couldn't stand the suspense anymore, the results were revealed.

Not only had Biddy Schumacher lost the election, she had lost it by a landslide. The Office of Distribution had gone to David Billingsworth, who, for all intents and purposes, had worked in the Town Hall since the age of 18 and had held several positions of political stature. Surprised and displaced by such a horrific defeat, Biddy locked herself up in her home for a week, not able to bear the looks people might give her as she passed. Her time inside was spent cutting out construction paper people. First those in the town, then those in the state, then those in the country, and finally those in the world were taped up all around her house like wall flowers, until Biddy had enough construction paper replicas to vote her in as President and Spiritual Leader of the Universe. Of course, it helped that she made sweeping campaign promises she knew she couldn't keep, like banning all scissors and glue. When she had consoled herself enough to leave home, she ran into Seth, who, for no reason at all, besides the fact that he wasn't anything, was standing in the middle of Biddy's block, watching his brown-shoed feet.

It was in that moment that Biddy, regenerated by a sudden burst of newfound optimism, asked Seth out on a date. It was a first for both. The date, which lasted for precisely three hours and forty-five minutes, consisted of dinner at the Fitzburge home—roasted lamb with mint jelly, pan-seared green beans in a light hollandaise sauce adorned by dill-seasoned boiled new potatoes—which Mrs. Eloise Fitzburge cooked and served, but did not attend. Due to Seth's general awkwardness and Biddy's lack of experience in holding substantial conversations with anyone she encountered, their dinner banter went something like this:

Biddy: "This lamb is good."

Seth: "My mother is a good cook. You should taste her onion bhajis."

Biddy: "My mother—may God rest her soul—used to cook in a toaster oven."

Seth: "I like toaster ovens. We have one. Mom won't let me use it."

This was followed up by a prolonged period of silence until Seth, who seemed to have been building up to his greatest compliment all night said, "I voted for you." Biddy looked up at him with wide eyes and wonderment. "So you're the one."

After they had eaten, Biddy and Seth adjourned to the garden and strolled around the backyard until they stopped to sit on the bench beside the hydrangeas. Under an early moonlight, Seth dared to take Biddy's hand in his. She let him. So was the success of their first date that it soon turned into a second and a third and a fourth and a fifth, until one night, while sitting on the porch swing in front of the Fitzburge home, Seth asked Biddy Schumacher to marry him. There was no reason for her not to accept.

The marriage was all that Hills Valley could talk about and everyone was in attendance, except for Padma. She had moved back home to Queens, New York, where she had been born and raised, leaving the town in utter shock as to why she would not want to live in Hills Valley anymore, thus causing them to lose their only Indian.

On the day of her wedding, Biddy Schumacher looked simply aglow. She was wearing her mother's wedding dress—may God rest her soul—also inherited, like the toaster oven. The wedding dress, which was several sizes too small for Biddy, was found in an old trunk along with the olive green, rusted, iron snack table and a gold and jewel embellished egg. Unable to find a Made in China sticker, and not needing such an elaborate piece of décor—after all, Easter came around only once a year—Biddy reckoned the egg might contain some value and brought it to Mr. McMillian who ran the town's antiques and collectibles shop. On every third weekend of the month—unless it was a holiday—Mr. McMillian held an auction out of the back room of his store, which had almost burned down the night the house/basket shop caught fire, and would have, had Mr. McMillian not hosed down his store earlier that day because it looked dirty.

The Auctioneer was astounded when Biddy showed him her egg. He confirmed her belief that the egg was worth money and wondered where in heaven she could have come across such an heirloom. Biddy, uncertain as ever, could only recall her mother—may God rest her soul—say she had once danced for the crowned heads of Europe. Intrigued,

Mr. McMillian assured Biddy he could sell the egg and sell it he did. The Fabergé Egg was bought by Hester Ester, Hills Valley's local historian and suspected Cold War Spy. Of course, the people of Hills Valley could never prove Hester's involvement, but her two lazy eyes and full-on mustache did little to dissuade suspicion. The egg, which Hester said connected her to her Russian heritage, sold for the total sum of eighty-thousand dollars. Biddy was thrilled. The very next week she bought her own house, which she paid for in cash—tens and twenties.

Seth moved into Biddy's home, where they lived together in complete matrimonial bliss for almost 30 years. Their routines, sometimes eerily similar, meshed well. They found no problem sharing a home or, as the case presented itself, a single bed. After all, the two were both quite slim. There were no children between them, despite the fact that the marriage was consummated in recognition with Catholic doctrine. Biddy and Seth's lovemaking occurred in the dark with their underclothes on and a sheet between them, for even these acts of nature Biddy could not bear to witness.

When it was evident that both were getting on in years, Biddy and Seth opted to adopt a cat—fluffy white with gray, black, and ginger. Magdalene was only fed cat food consisting of 100% meat, in accordance to Biddy's no fish rule. The cat, whose litter box was kept veiled in the bathroom, was taught how to open and close the bathroom door, as was Seth. He found it just a tad odd that every time he used the bathroom Biddy would lock herself in their bedroom until he was done. Nevertheless, neither Seth nor Biddy had a single complaint about the other and took full joy in the knowledge that they were, perhaps, made for each other.

Biddy outlived her husband, something that was not in

the least surprising since she was always the more active of the two. Believing that the soul lived on, Biddy was certain that Seth—may God rest his soul—not only looked down on her, but was happily at peace since there was no way that the good Lord would let her husband spend all eternity with that face. Biddy's only concern, and one she broached with Father O'Malley on several occasions, was whether she would recognize her husband when she finally joined him in Heaven. Father, who was a very patient man on account of his vice for bourbon, brandy and sacramental wine, assured Biddy she would. Still, it was a sad time for her and Magdalene, who had become very attached to Seth—may God rest his soul. Seth always believed it was his gentle nature that the cat recognized and cared for. Biddy believed it to be the scent of the medicated ointment Seth applied daily to his face that caused him to be the cat's favorite.

In her last days, all Biddy's memories began to fade and her sense of reality started to slip. She was unable to care for the cat on her own. Due to the impressive talent the cat had acquired from learning to open and close the bathroom door, turn the lights on and off and, after Seth's death—may God rest his soul—flush the toilet, she was taken in by a band of clowns from Moscow, who used her in their traveling theatre. Yet, despite Biddy's weakening, every night and every morning when she looked upon that faded, glass-encased image of herself casting the vote, Biddy Schumacher-Fitzburge remembered that day precisely as if it was happening again, for the very first time.

A Shade of Grey

Emma blew out the smoke with some force. It was, in fact, the most forceful thing she'd done all day. She began to play with the hem of her skirt. It scalloped along the edge and she liked how its silky texture felt between her fingers.

"Can I get you anything else, miss?"

She looked up at the waiter and stared at him for a long moment before she replied.

"I'll have a martini please. Make it dirty. No, wait. Make it watermelon. Actually, if I'm going towards the sweeter side, maybe I should just have apple? Yes, I'll have an appletini, please."

"Are you sure about that?"

"Uh, huh."

"An appletini it is then."

The waiter walked away to fetch Emma's drink; she fidgeted with the table settings.

The restaurant Emma was sitting in sported only candles and backlighting to enhance its dimness. The walls were painted mauve with a layered texture that made it look very much like the petal formation on a dark, pink rose. The dusty white distressed wooden floors repeated every footstep, making Emma antsier. Glancing at her watch for about the twelfth time that evening, she drew the cigarette to her pale-pink painted lips and inhaled deeply. She could hardly believe she had once thought of quitting; now she thought of nothing but her next smoke. A half-burned cigarette in one hand, she reached out for her handbag with the other. Pulling out a pack of cigarettes, she checked to see how many were left. *Shit*, she thought, *only half a pack*, not enough to get her through this evening.

For a split second she fathomed leaving and putting off the whole thing until another day, or another year even, but she knew she couldn't; it wasn't right. This had to be dealt with now. Emma dropped the pack back into her bag and pulled out her compact. Checking her reflection in the mirror, she thought about her color choice in makeup this evening. Richard always liked her in more subtle tones. "Quiet Colors," he called them. Emma preferred more "noisy" shades. Even in her dress she preferred something more hip, trendy, edgy, while Richard favored a conservative look. She wondered what Richard ever saw in her to begin with. She certainly didn't look the way she did tonight when they had first met. Where had they first met? She couldn't remember. At some party perhaps, it had to be — or maybe in a bar? No, Richard didn't frequent bars. Too much smoke, too much noise. "*Too much life*," Emma added aloud to herself, clicking the compact shut.

"Appletini."

The voice startled her and she jumped as a small gasp escaped her lips.

"I'm sorry. You startled me. I didn't know you had come back."

"That's okay, miss. Is there anything else I can get you?"

"No, thank you."

The waiter nodded and went on to another table.

Emma put out her cigarette and took a sip of the apple

martini. Placing the drink on the table, she rested her French manicured hands near it. The white cotton/poly blended tablecloth felt rough to the touch.

"Hey sweetie, sorry I'm late," a tranquil voice said. Coming around Emma and sitting down across the table, Richard scraped his chair against the floor.

"Oh, that's fine, Richard, at least you're here now," she smiled.

"You wouldn't believe what happened at work today. This crazy old lady came in and …"

Emma blocked out Richard's banter as he continued to speak. She had become good at doing that. Emma watched Richard's face as he went on and on about something inanely boring or unimportant. Her face kept an interested expression while her eyes screamed of death. She wondered if he ever bothered to look into her eyes to see what was going on inside of her.

How had she ever let the relationship get this far? Because she loved him was her only answer. She loved him because he was different than all of the other men in her life. Richard wasn't emotionally distant; he expressed his love for her, his desire to be with her. Richard made her feel special, he involved Emma in every part of his life, he treated her like — actually — he treated her like a pet! This realization hit Emma, and it was true. She had never thought of it that way. She was his pet. He pampered her when she was good and scolded her when she did something he thought was wrong, like smoking. She couldn't believe that all this time she never saw it.

Emma always had the feeling that something was off in the relationship. At first she contributed it to never being in a relationship with such a great guy before. Then later on she began to sense the awkward feeling coming from the smothering, but now she knew exactly what the feeling stemmed from. She was Richard's pet — or better yet — his project. She had to be! *Look at me*, she thought! *My make-up, my hair, my clothes, all for him, no, all him!* Emma focused her eyes on Richard and she fell. She loved him, she did. But she knew she had to do what needed to be done. She just didn't want to hurt him. He may have treated her like his pet, his personal possession to sculpt and mold into his own version of perfection, but Richard didn't do it to hurt her, and she knew that.

"Wow, that's just … something," Emma plastered an even wider smile on her face; Richard had finished speaking.

"So, I was thinking that maybe this weekend we could escape someplace romantic?"

This was it. This was the time; she had to tell him. Emma took a deep breath. She kept staring at him with that plastered smile on her face. All the ways she could possibly tell him it was over ran through her mind evolving and dissolving each time a better phrase came to her. There was too much time lapsing; she had to speak; she had to say something. Which phrase should she use? Which statement was right?

"Richard, it's over!" And it came out just like that, surprising her with her own bluntness.

"What?"

"It's over. We're over. I'm sorry. I've been trying to tell you for some time now but I just couldn't and I didn't want it to come out this way either. I had thought we'd sit down and have a nice dinner, some conversation, drinks; I'd have a pack of cigarettes, you'd tell me to quit and I'd say, 'I can't. I'm addicted.' And then you'd say in that corny singsong voice, 'I'm addicted to love,' and we'd both start laughing and

I'd tell you I loved you and then we'd share a sweet kiss and when that was over I'd look into your beautiful, warm brown eyes and say we needed to talk and that's when I would tell you that I wanted to break up, but that's not how it happened and I'm sorry, I'm so sorry, but I just couldn't... I can't do this anymore."

"You can't do what anymore? Love me? Talk to me? Tell me how you're feeling? I'm extremely confused here. Why is this so ... all of a sudden?"

"It's not all of a sudden, Richard. I've known for some time that this wasn't right, that we weren't right. It wasn't until tonight that I finally began to really understand why, but Richard ... I love you, I still do. I just can't do this anymore. I wanted to and I tried but it had to be over because ... It just has to be over."

"That's not a reason and I won't accept it as one. I love you, baby, and I'll do whatever it takes, I'll make it all right, I promise. Just tell me what and I'll do it."

"Oh Richard, no. It can't work that way."

"Why not!?"

Emma stopped. She couldn't answer him. There was no way she would be able to tell Richard he just wasn't enough for her. She may have loved him, and he may have loved her, but Richard didn't give Emma what she needed, what she deserved. Emma always felt stifled with Richard. She tried so hard to live up to what he expected her to be, what he thought she was. But Emma wasn't that woman. She tried to be his vision because she loved him and she honestly thought he was the guy she could spend the rest of her life with. But Emma didn't want that.

She needed to be free and she needed a man who understood and appreciated her independence, her inconsistencies, and her neurotic tendencies. Emma couldn't be kept by Richard, or by any man. She would be nobody's pet. But how could she tell Richard all this? He was so sensitive, so loving, perhaps too loving. Richard loved her too much for his own good. She couldn't hurt him like that. Emma fumbled in her bag for another cigarette and, putting it to her lips, lit it.

"You should quit smoking. It's really not good for you."

"I can't. I'm addicted."

"*I'm addicted to love.*"

Neither of them laughed.

"I do love you. I just can't be with you. I know you want this great explanation as to why, but I don't have one for you. I may never have one for you. Just know that I can't do this anymore. I can't do us anymore."

"You just can't walk out on me, Emma! I need an explanation. Goddamn it! I've done everything I can in this relationship to show you my love, to show you my support and you pull this shit with me!"

"Bull. What support have you shown me, Richard?"

"I accept your smoking, when you know I don't like it."

"No, you don't! If you accepted it, you wouldn't keep throwing it in my face."

"I do not."

"Yes you do. You've never accepted my smoking. Even when you said you were okay with it, you never were. I'm sorry that I smoke; I can't help it. It's a part of me and you can't accept that. This whole relationship I tried to be what you wanted because I loved you, but you want too much, Richard. I can't give you what you want, it's not who I am. But then again, you don't even know who I am."

"I know perfectly well who you are!"

"Then who am I?"

Richard couldn't answer. Whether it was, the absurdity of the question or whether he really didn't know who she was, Emma wasn't sure, but she wouldn't sit there until he figured the answer out. Emma had already given Richard too much of her time.

Emma pushed her chair back, acutely aware of it scraping against the hard wood floor. She grabbed her bag and got up. Taking one last drag off her cigarette she leaned over the table and her eyes caught Richard's. They told her nothing. They were blank and searching at the same time. Without flinching and without even a whisper, she crushed her cigarette out in the glass ashtray and walked away, the familiar trail of smoke lingering behind her.

And it always intrigued me how it loomed out of nowhere and how anyone could possibly mistake it for anything except for exactly what it was. Every time I rounded that corner by Exit 25 on the Hutch there it was, catching my attention. I always thought it was more of a distraction, looking the way it did now, than it would be if it had kept its natural appearance. I'm almost positive it would have gone unnoticed if not for its apparent disguise.

Even though I'd seen it time and time again, there was something about this particular night that made it more absorbing than before. It was late, really late, sometime around two or three in the morning. It was one of those nights that are crisp—clean and cold, but not yet winter. I was driving back from a party at Purchase in my Maxima with my friend Barry Longdin, who was fast asleep or passed out in my passenger seat. Either one was fine with me. My other friend Chuck Scalary was in my back seat fucking this girl he met at the party and who he wanted to bring home with him. I tried keeping my eyes on the road instead of in the rearview mirror watching what was happening in the back. Lucky for me, or maybe not, it was also one of those nights when no one's on the road, giving me no need to check my mirror. I always preferred that type of night; it seemed more peaceful. I was quite accustomed to driving that late at night with all the carousing my friends and I did. We usually took turns driving, depending on what event we're going to. Tonight was all me.

I was originally supposed to go up to Purchase last week for their Fall Ball, but the weather had been less then favorable. I decided not to chance it and stayed home instead. Because I had missed the Ball, I promised my friend Sam that I would go to the next function her college was throwing, which turned out to be tonight. I asked Barry if he wanted to come along with me. The idea of attending anything at Purchase really didn't sit well with him at first. Barry was totally opposed to the thought of going to a fag party, as he called it. Despite Barry's blatant homophobia, I didn't want to attend alone so I simply informed him that the place would be filled with plenty of straight girls for him to get with since they were around gay guys all the time and would surely welcome a stud like himself. That seemed to change his mind, though he was still slightly hesitant. I quickly added that those gay guys didn't like jocks and that's why they were at an art school, for good measure. Truthful or not, it sealed the deal. With Barry ready to roll, I was able to drag Chuck along on the same premise, only I didn't have to try so hard on the convincing part. Chuck isn't gay, but the boy has a huge ego. I knew he wouldn't be able to stay away from a party where tons of gay guys would be ogling him, at least if he thought they would. I sometimes think Chuck would fuck just about anything on two legs, female or male, if he was horny enough and he believed they wanted him badly, which was always. As for myself, I don't mind the gays. They don't bother me and I don't bother them.

The party itself was okay. I was able to find my friend Sam among the swarm of dancing and drinking college kids.

I introduced Sam to both Barry and Chuck and I could see how both guys were hot for her. Fortunately for Sam, she had a boyfriend in some Florida university I can never remember the name of. I left the boys to fend for themselves and hung out with Sam and her Purchase friends. I have to say they were all pretty cool. Some were a little weird. Okay a lot were weird. Well, compared to how normal Sam is anyway. I actually had a nice time. I would have stayed a while longer but I found Barry totally wasted. I figured I should get Barry out of there before he wound up in a position he wouldn't be too happy with in the morning. I didn't get any objections about leaving from Chuck who had become permanently attached to the girl who was now in my back seat moaning from whatever Chuck was doing to her.

I turned my head to look at Barry. He had started a slow drool on himself. I was glad it wasn't on my car. The moaning noises from the girl Chuck picked up started to get louder. The sounds were accompanied by Chuck's aggressive grunting. I quickly turned up the radio that had been on an almost silent volume. A U2 song came across the air, the one that Cher opens all her concerts with. Don't ask me how I know that, I just do. As I listened to the song, I couldn't ever recall actually hearing Cher's version on the radio. I started to wonder if Cher actually ever recorded the song or if she only sang it in her concerts. Then I started to wonder if I was going crazy because I couldn't believe I was even thinking about it. Maybe I had spent too much time at Purchase or maybe I was just tired of listening to Chuck bang in the back. Whatever the case, I started paying close attention to the song's lyrics.

As I listened I realized that even though I'd heard the song many times before, I never knew what the lyrics actually said. I don't know exactly why, but the lyrics began to transfix me. It might have been the night or the fact that I was driving on the Hutch. The Hutch seems to sooth me; it's almost as if nothing bad can happen to me on the Hutch because it's the road home. I'm not sure why, but what I am sure of is that the lyrics made me see my life. I saw the relationships I've had with girls and what my friends and I do on the weekends and I saw how it is always the same. Barry is always drunk and Chuck is always pumping some girl he'll never see again and I'm always driving home alone because my relationships are built on weak ground because I'm looking for them in the wrong places and in the wrong people. In fact, my entire life has been one big search for something I haven't found because I have no idea what I've been looking for.

The song ended but my thoughts didn't. I don't know why this all came about now but it did and I realized I needed to do something about it. I didn't want to keep living my life searching for things and never finding them. I didn't want to keep lying to myself about liking what I'd been doing. I didn't like it. I didn't like any of it. I needed to change.

I looked up at the approaching road sign and notice that it was the exit I was supposed to take. Exit 12 on the Hutch. I got off the exit and rode around the ramp to the stoplight. I realized that if I turned left I'd be heading towards my ex-girlfriend's house. We dated for a long time and the sex was awesome, but I couldn't deal with her heavy pot smoking anymore and I had to let her go. I know that if I had stayed with her our relationship would have really gotten fucked up. I sometimes felt that she loved her pot more than she ever loved me. The light changed and I made the right towards Barry's home. He lives in Pelham as does Chuck. The first stop I made was at Barry's house. I pulled into his driveway and stopped the car. I tried to wake him but it didn't work as well as I hoped. He stirred a bit but he was in no condition to get out of the car himself. I called to Chuck in the back and told him he had to help me dump Barry on his doorstep. Chuck bitched a little but I quickly reminded him that the sooner we did this the sooner he could screw the girl with him in more positions than my car allowed. It was no time before we had gotten Barry to his front door. I opened it with his key and we walked him into his living room and left him on the couch. Chuck was annoyed that I didn't just dump him outside but that I made him help me carry Barry into the house. I told Chuck to zip his fly because his limp dick was dangling out of it. He just smirked and grabbed it.

We got back in the car and I started for his home. A few minutes later I had dropped off Chuck and the girl and they continued their sexual adventures all the way up the walk and into the house. I sat in the empty car for a moment before I turned around and headed back for the Hutch. I was alone now. My friends were gone and I didn't miss them at all. I was actually glad to be rid of them. I had been thinking about the change I needed and wondered how I would make it. As I turned to head back north I stopped the car and turned around. I knew that if I went south I would end up in New York City. The Hutch would end and I'd have no choice but to get on whatever road came next.

As I drove towards the end of the Hutch, I thought about how safe it made me feel. It was almost representative of my life. I felt safe and familiar with it and therefore never tried to change it. That wasn't the case anymore. I didn't know exactly where I was heading or where I would end up but I kept driving towards the end finally understanding why

I was so intrigued by that looming object near Exit 25. It was like me, masquerading as something else just to fit in its environment. I had been doing the same all along. I didn't belong with Barry and Chuck, I wasn't at all like them, and I didn't belong with any of the girls I've dated. I didn't know where I did belong but I was going to find out.

I was far away from my home now, far from my life, from Exit 25 and that cell phone tower disguised as a pine tree.

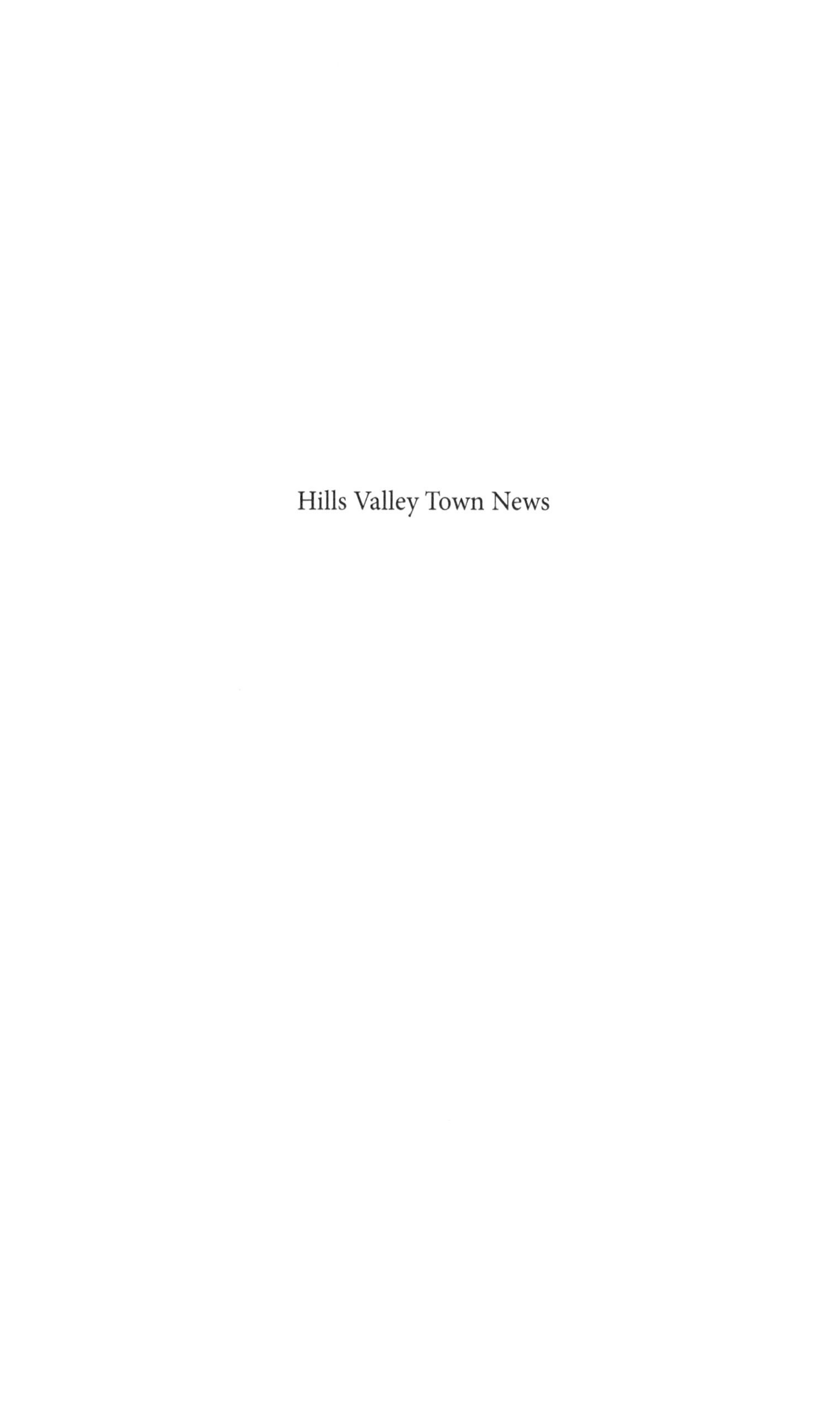

Hills Valley Town News

vote BIDDY SCHUMACHER
OF
Office of Distribution
Hills Valley
David Billingsworth
Getting the Job Done!

Local Election A Real Thumper
Schumacher and Billingsworth face off for Office of
Distribution

By Roger Kranzden, Political Reporter

When Niles Nillsman died at the ripe age of 84 leaving
the post of Office of Distribution available for the taking,
not a soul in Hills Valley suspected the young and popular
David Billingsworth would have any contention when he
announced his bid to run for the position. But when late-
to-the-race candidate Biddy Schumacher tossed her well
intentioned hat in the ring, the citizens of Hills Valley were
in utter awe.

It is safe to say that David Billingsworth is favored to
win. He's held numerous offices within the town government
his entire adult life. Hills Valley residents will recall when, at
the age of 16, David painted the first fence ever to be erected
around Town Hall. The Mayor thought he showed immense
initiative and when David came of age he was hired as the
Mayor's personal aid. Billingsworth has been moving up the
political ladder ever since.

Little is known about Schumacher's desire to fill the
post. She has never held office in Hills Valley, nor has she

ever contributed greatly to the town at large. She can be seen attending rummage sales and charity fairs conducted by the numerous religious organizations Hills Valley is proud of. But aside from quietly working away at her job at Hills Valley Power, Water and Paper, the town's largest employer, Biddy's ambitions for anything more were never shown. She is, we may add, the daughter of Fladora Schumacher, who was a prominent citizen of Hills Valley and a great contributor financially to the town. While there is resounding affection for Fladora, will it be enough to get her daughter elected to Office of Distribution?

"She has moral standing," said Father O'Malley, head of Our Lord and Savior, Catholic Church. "A dedicated parishioner for years. Very in touch with her religion."

When Billingsworth was asked about his own moral standing, he had this to say: "Religion and Politics have no business going to the dance together. My track record in local government speaks for itself. I have served the people of Hills Valley well, and I will continue to serve the people after they elect me to Office of Distribution." It may be important to note that David Billingsworth is a Lutheran.

When we reached out to the other candidate for comment on the issues, what we received was very interesting. "God wants me to run for Office of Distribution. If He did not, I would not have found the note I made to myself to run."

Elections will be held this coming Tuesday at Town Hall per usual. The outcome of this vote should prove most interesting.

Brian Centrone is the author of two short story collections: *I Voted for Biddy Schumacher: Mismatched Tales from the Mind of Brian Centrone* and *Erotica*, and of the debut novel, *An Ordinary Boy*. Four of his one-act plays, including *Hills Valley's First Fence*—a prequel to "The Life and Times of Biddy Schumacher"— have been produced on the stage for The National Endowment for the Arts' *The Big Read*. He has an MA in Novel Writing from The University of Manchester (UK). Brian is also an award-winning professor of writing and literature in New York. Visit Brian at www. briancentrone.com.

luke kurtis is an interdisciplinary artist focusing on the intersection of photography, writing, and design. He has exhibited work in galleries and alternative spaces around the country. His work has also appeared in *The Emerson Review, Encounters, Georgia Backroads, Iceland Review, Palaver, The Red Truck Review, Skin To Skin,* and *S/tick: Feminists on Guard,* among other places. He lives and works in New York City's Greenwich Village. Visit luke at bd-studios.com.